Legend of Dabi

Volume One

DoDeHi

Copyright © 2024

All rights reserved.

All rights reserved by Mocha Mint Publishing and Mahogany Ann. No part of this publication may be reproduced, distributed, or transmitted in any form or by any means, including photocopying, recording, or other electronic or mechanical methods, without the author's prior written permission, except in the case of brief quotations embodied in critical reviews and certain other non-commercial uses permitted by copyright law.

Contents

Dedication i

Acknowledgments.. ii

About the Author iii

Prelude Eden's Hope.. 2

Chapter 1 Prism Beginnings 14

Chapter 2 Wilderness Crimes 31

Chapter 3 Ride Of Resistance 47

Short Story Elsu Hania.. 61

Dedication

I dedicate this book and all its success to my Lord and Savior, Jesus Christ, who has sustained my health to write the Legend of Dabi Series. I also would like to dedicate this series to Elizabeth Limon, my fiancé and soon-to-be future wife. I thank God for her encouragement, support, and patience.

Acknowledgments

I would like to acknowledge and thank Amazon Publishing for providing me the opportunity to publish as a first-time author. I would also like to acknowledge and thank Matthew Evans, the senior book consultant, Kevin Paul, the project manager, and the rest of the team who have helped the creation of Legend of Dabi come true.

About the Author

Dorian D. Hill was born and raised in Southfield, Michigan. As a child, Dorian had an amazing imagination to escape the harsh reality of being bedridden due to his chronic illness, which inspired him to do what only his body could manage, and that was to create fantasy and dramatic storytelling. Now as a healthy adult, Dorian dreamed of seeing his storytelling published and inspiring his readers for the same sense of thrilling escape from reality as he did when he was a child.

Prelude
Eden's Hope

A pulsating abyss of space that strokes an aurora canvas and a prism of colors. The vibrant colors twinkle immense little stars in the heavens to author rising stars on earth. As the dust of vibrant little stars twinkles and dwindles, a transition in time reveals a round stone that expands and quakes into the center of the world. The stone is mighty and formed with crystallized colors of pearl skies, ocean blues, country greens, and bronze lands. From the depths of its mountains and rocky wilderness, the stone elevates to the sunrise by polypropylene three-strand rope and a treadwheel crane.

The stone, in all its glory, sways high above the clouds and within the breeze. It is revered by a small excavation team of natives in a rocky wilderness. Native men and women of Tishbe, Eden, cheer. The women cry with joy, and the men shake hands. Eventually, the premature celebration is over, and it is time to pull their native cowboy hats back over their sweaty faces. The small native excavation teams are determined to safely retrieve the stone for the drop site in the far distance.

Dabi Hakan operates the treadwheel crane and continues the rise of the stone.

> "Run, Dabi." the overseer shouts in eagerness as he admires the stone's glistening shower.

Dabi crawls on his hands and knees, struggling to catch his breath. His vision is blurry, and his stomach is nauseous. He is overwhelmed by the hot climate of the wilderness. His immature dreadlock hair, scrawny muscles, and sticky clothing are drenched in sweat. Unable to regain the stamina and willpower to operate the treadwheel crane again, the glistening stone remains suspended in the clouds and in the breeze. His core is aching, especially his quads and buttocks. The force to operate the treadwheel crane is unbearable due to the sheer size and weight of the stone. A single lunge felt like hundreds of pounds. Dabi managed this far, but the thought of failing Eden's pardon agitates his focus and confidence.

> "Now, Dabi!" the overseer shouts once more, but this time he is crass because of the uncertainty of the rope and crane.

The native excavation team, men and women, are suddenly afflicted with great stress. The women glare towards the treadwheel crane with their hands locked together, and the men hold their heads in disbelief. Moments pass, and Dabi is lost in his thoughts. His mind wanders into a limbo prayer where tranquil ripples of water remind him of the many suffering memories he has encountered in Eden. Every fleeting memory evaporates one after another.

A memory drips and ripples in the water in Dabi's state mind of a promiscuous woman – shameful and dishonorable to a prideful native people. Her slightly above-knee-length skirt is ripped to her thighs, and her fitted buttoned-down blouse is torn to her breast. She did not stink, but her soul had an odor with an unnatural smile. Her face was like the masks of ancient theatre. She grieves and mourns, but her sinister face is very amused. Dabi, unsettling, struggles to maneuver on top of the water's surface as he reaches to save her, but only contacts with her mist.

The promiscuous woman's memory evaporates as another memory splashes in the distance and ripples in the water in Dabi's state of mind. He seeks the memory of a seasoned man. The man has lost most of his hair with only spots of thinning strands of hair remaining on his head. His body is ill, his skin complexion is fading, and his bony ribs bulge. One side of his eyes is angry, and lifeless, and his mouth, with a new set of animalistic teeth, rends to his ear. His other eye is sorrowful and more human than the other. On his left hand, his material ring is damaged, and on his right hand, he grasps the head of a severed bloody teddy bear. Dabi's focus zooms on the man and fears his transforming appearance and the unknown tragedy of the teddy bear's severed bloody head.

Suddenly, the stone, like a burning sun, burst through an ocean, fiery sky. It is crashing rapidly and breaking sound barriers to the magnitude you feel the vibrations. The man's memory is burned into an evaporation, and Dabi huddles in terror. As Dabi huddles to the water's surface beneath him, he is haunted by many ghostly apparitions yearning for him as they drown. The stone is nearing and ready to plunge Dabi into the haunted waters.

> "No!" Dabi shouts as he opens his eyes with determination. No more of his native people to become victims to the totem of owls.

Compelled, Dabi releases himself from his huddle and spins around to face the fiery crashing stone. He catches the stone with his bare hands, that quickly becomes engulfed by the stone's flames. With great struggle, Dabi is steadfast on top of the water's surface like muddy ground. Dabi's ignited willpower and the crashing stone are in a gridlock. Winds explode, and waterspouts emerge one after another all around Dabi and the stone. Their war creates a storm, and thunder and lightning consume everything.

Dabi is jolted and gasps back in the rocky wilderness. His vision is returning, his body is confident, and ringing voices are easing.

> "What are you doing, Dabi? Get up now!" the overseer's demands are clear.

Dabi rises to drive through the pain, takes in a deep breath, and exhales. He takes a single lunge that bares an intense muscular contraction. Wood begins to creak, the crane begins to squeak, and finally, the treadwheel crane budges. The native men and women's great stress is alleviating. Dabi takes a second lunge and begins baby steps on the treadwheel crane till he takes off into an epic sprint. His efforts are achieving the satisfaction and admiration of the overseer and the other natives.

Dabi and the native excavation team burdensomely navigate the stone for safe passage through sharp and narrow corners, harmful cliffs, and jagged edges in the rocky wilderness. Now, the stone is admired by the sun. The eight native men on the ground ready themselves to take the rope that rotates the crane horizontally towards the drop site. Dabi falls to his knees again, exhausted, but this time with an accomplished smile on his face. The eight native men tug the rope numerously but fail to pull successfully.

"One, two, three, pull!" the eight native men shout in unison.

The eight native men continue to count in unison and tug repetitiously but fail repetitiously.

"Oh, Great Spirit, this is embarrassing," the overseer is unimpressed.

The eight native men are anxious and almost discouraged by the overseer's sullen expression and stiff posture. Losing count, the eight native men attempt another try.

> "Okay. Come, now!" the lead native man attempts to encourage the other seven native men behind him. "One, two, three, pull!"

The encouraged eight native men to yank the rope into, and finally, a successful four-step pull closer to the drop site. Dabi is satisfied as the stone rumbles away from him, the native woman yelps excitably, and the overseer exhales relief. The eight native men continue to yank and pull another four steps closer to the drop site. However, the wood is creaking louder, and the crane is squeaking and weakling the loudest. The eight native men are doing well with another successful yank and pull, but now six steps closer to the drop site. Concerning, one of the native women catches a slight off-balance in Dabi's direction and the faint lowering of the stone.

Dabi rests within the treadwheel crane until he subtly feels vibrations throughout his body like a relaxing massage. He shifts his attention to observe the small debris bouncing around him. Dabi slowly sits up cautiously in the now unstable treadwheel crane. One of the native women runs to another native woman to discuss the subtle off-balance as she refers to written diagrams, mechanical engineering, geological outliers, and possible mathematical errors.

> "What the hell is that noise?" The overseer is startled.

The sounds of wood creaking and crane weakling have reached a climatic disturbance. The stone's sheer size echoes throughout the rocky wilderness and weighs down the mountains. The native women of three accompany the overseer to predict a storm of events. The overseer signals and alarms for the eight native men to cease; unfortunately, they cannot hear him. The eight native men continue to yank and pull, successfully, another six steps closer to the drop site.

"Get them to stop. Hurry!" The overseer is uneased.

The overseer instructs one of the native women to report the news to the eight native men. She runs and runs into what feels like a new atmosphere and fears she will never make it in time. Her breathing becomes labored, and she can only hear her decreasing heartbeat. The objective eludes her, becoming farther and farther away as she watches the eight native men achieve a steady pace of pulling the rope. Eventually, she accomplishes her goal.

"Stop!" the native woman screams at the eight native men.

Tragically, like the sound of a single fired shot from a revolver to the sky, the rope snaps. Whiplashed, Dabi endures and quickly leaps out of the collapsing treadwheel crane. Hidden birds in the mountains fly away from their nests, and critters on land burrow in the ground and run inside small tunnels. The stone sways wildly, destroying all the tallest mountains in the rocky wilderness. Mountain rubble showers the cratering ground like falling meteors.

The falling impact disperses the eight native men on the ground and impales the native woman who runs to warn them. Two of the native men fall into a crater's pit. One native man hangs onto the edge for his life while struggling to pull himself up since the second native man is clinging to his leg.

> "Let go of me!" the hanging native man mournfully pleads to the native man clinging to his leg.

> "Please save me!" the second native man crying for help while clinging to the hanging native man's leg.

As mountain rubble continues to shower the cratering ground, the last two fearful native women flee, but the other six native men rush towards the two hanging native men's rescue. The stone sways chaotically and continues to destroy smaller mountains as it descends. Dabi subtly hears fabric ripping. It is the rope. Dabi immediately scans it until the stone takes a sharp plunge above the eight native men. Dabi's end of the rope swiftly runs towards the edge of the mountain like a rabbit.

> "Shit!" Dabi exclaims as he jolts to catch the escaping rope from running off the cliff and stopping the crushing demise of the eight native men below him.

Dabi is at the end of the rope. His hands are gripping the rope tightly. Desperately trying to prevent being dragged off the edge of the mountain by the weight of the stone, Dabi slides and kicks up dirt and dust. The palms of his hands begin to bleed by the lacerated friction of the stone's pull. He quickly ponders a plan to save the eight native men below and himself.

> "Let the rope go, Dabi!" the overseer uncovers himself from the showering rubble and debris.

Bewildered, Dabi is conflicted with the judgment of the overseer. If he lets go of the rope now, the eight native men will perish. Dabi suffers physically and mentally to ensure the best outcome. From the highest mountain in the rocky wilderness, Dabi finds the area on the ground to drop the stone. If he coordinates the timing perfectly by releasing the rope, it will fall away from the eight native men and into a crater's pit.

> "No, Dabi!" The overseer shouts. "If you destroy that stone, you will keep Eden in its curse."

Conflicted, Dabi is losing time. The stone's momentum is decelerating and still above the eight native men struggling to escape the crater's pit and the unstable terrain. The longer Dabi clashes with the thoughts of the overseer, the palms of his hands become severely lacerated to the extent that his blood drenches the end of the rope and drips to the ground. Furthermore, the longer Dabi clashes with the thoughts of the overseer, the stone's chaotic sway continues to destroy lowering mountains as it descends. Tragically, another mountain rubble falls, but this time, it plunges the second native man into the mouth of the crater's pit.

Dabi is devastated. He has been tempted by hesitation that has cost a native man's life and the mourning of the surviving native men. Now, the blood on his lacerated hands feels worse. The overseer is amused that the stone is almost free from destruction and within his grasp. Dabi is determined to save everyone else and to clash with the overseer's judgment. Unfortunately, the stone has decelerated to a halt and hangs to a calm, deathly descent. The overseer forsakes his crew and prepares to retrieve the stone and its glistening power. Dabi's willpower to endure is ignited again. He desires to accelerate the stone again, but he must bear its sheer size.

Dabi strains as he pulls the rope higher up the mountain. Bearing the burden of the stone's sheer size, Dabi's feet struggle as he now slides in his own blood as it runs down his wrists. His nose bleeds, and his eyes rupture. The stone's intense and sudden crash against the mountains forces the overseer's striking reaction and resentful awe.

> "Damn you, Dabi" the overseer contempt.

Dabi is at a tug of war on the count of three where he aims to let go of the rope and save the seven remaining native men. The overseer glares as he observes stone is, unbelievably, under Dabi's control. The native men rescued the hanging native man from the crater's pit, unfortunately, they have all lost the time to escape from under the stone's eclipse. Dabi pulls the stone effectively on the first count while the seven native men congregate and pray for their lives. The stone swaying above their bodies feels like a shade of their last moments. On the second count, the overseer clenches his fists maliciously, because the stone is revered to rebuke the curse over Eden, but Dabi is willing to destroy it. At last, the third count. Dabi, in all his might, lets go of the rope from his grasp and zips down the mountain. The high-pitch zipping increases the further the stone plummets to the craters. The crashing stone earthquakes the rocky wilderness, bringing the seven native men to their praying faces, the overseer to his knees, and Dabi braced to a balance.

The seven native men tremble as their heads and necks are shielded by their arms. The ground comes to a calmness, and one by one, the seven native men examine their bodies, awestruck they remain alive. They glance upon the mountain to Dabi's grieving sacrifice with eyes, hearts, and hands of gratitude. However, the overseer knocks off pointy rubble on each side of his head and crushes it with his bare hands at the sight of the stone destroyed, the native's praises, and Dabi standing.

Chapter 1
Prism Beginnings

It is early in the morning. A young teacher enters the kindergarten classroom of twenty students. Her round glasses capture trust and innocence like a porcupine. Her slightly above-knee length skirt reveals her carefree and light-hearted character like a bird, and her fitted buttoned-down blouse benefits her figure and fertility like a peacock. She places her leather-brown bag of assignments on her desk with subtle, weary eyes but takes a deep breath to serve her students with grace.

"Good morning, class," the teacher bestows.

"Good morning, Ms. Wapeka," the classroom wecomes her.

Ms. Wapeka's inviting smile briefly becomes troubled in a decay of thought after greeting her students. However, she shrugs and casts off her distracting demeanor. As soon as her claustrophobic moment departs from her, she reconciles with a new agenda of the hour. Her second thoughts drop a handful of assignments on her desk. She was primarily prepared to teach from her brown leather bag. Getting her hands dirty from white chalk, she writes the agenda on the blackboard.

She opens her desk drawer and obtains various colored paper, stickers, crayons, markers, and colored pencils. Passing every item to every student, she carefully explains the spontaneous assignment to the classroom. Allowing the classroom adequate time to complete their personal assignment, Ms. Wapeka sits in her chair and participates with her students.

Time passes, and Ms. Wapeka stands in front of her desk to share the things she has decorated on her colored paper of stickers, markers, crayons, and colored pencils. She illustrates golden and silver star stickers that are placed on the upper right-hand corner and some on the left side of her black-colored paper. With crayons, she has drawn a sun that takes up the entire upper left-hand corner of her black-colored paper. In the center foreground of the black-colored paper is a prism drawn with colored pencils. Flames of crayons consume the left side of the prism, and refined colors of white and gray outline the inner prism-like reflective glass. Finally, colorful marker smears of brown, blue, red, purple, pink, green, and yellow are drawn from within the prism and throughout the rest of the black-colored paper.

Ms. Wapeka glides her fingers across her illustrations as she begins concepts of darkness and light, black and white, dreams and totems. Like a lantern in the darkness, her interpretation charms all her students' wide, golden little eyes and jaw-dropping inspiration. Her fingers start with the burning sun on her black colored paper.

> "This is our Great spirit," Ms. Wapeka touched the sun.

Her gliding fingers continue to elaborate her illustrating tale to a point where she lightly strokes her concepts and fantasizes them all. She entertains that the Great Spirit blessed Eden with attributes of wisdom, dreams, and power as her fingers gently stroked for the stars.

> "These are our mystical totems," Ms. Wapeka claims in wonder.

Ms. Wapeka indulges in reminiscing that the totems guide Eden through despair and to prosperity. If chosen, a native will experience the attributes and personal assignment of their destined totem. She pauses for a moment to approach her desk, but this time, she opens a different drawer. Grasping a wooden deer figurine. Ms. Wapeka returns to the front of her desk.

> "This is my totem," Ms. Wapeka shares with excitement.

Ms. Wapeka grasps her wooden deer totem intimately as she shares a story about when she once was tiny, like her students. Angeni Wapeka was orphaned at such an early age and without guidance, or so she thought. Her frustrations provoked her to flee the orphanage and liberate herself in the forest. She coddled inside the death of a fallen tree to cry and pray for the family to come. After hours of crying and praying, she would fall asleep until the death of the fallen tree struck above her. Freighted, she hesitates to open her eyes. She crawls to the end of the opening of the fallen dead tree to peek outside and discover something so angelic.

Her tiny little eyes could not comprehend. It was a deer shrouded in a cold blue and white fog. Its silhouette antlers harmonized with all the trees of the forest and its eyes were bright like the light of a lighthouse. Angeni's heart encouraged her to exit from within her fallen dead tree and miles to the deer. Her courage guided her far until she reached the deer. Finally, when she was only small fingers away with her tiny little arms, the deer was not so big, and it calmed her. She pets the deer on the head, but it sparkles and flees.

Rescue natives find Angeni standing alone in the forest with her arms, yearning for the vanished deer. They gently carried her away back to the orphanage. Awestruck, her hopeful, tiny little eyes never forgot the spot of her fleeting encounter of peace and clarity in the forest. Now, as an adult, Angeni's passion for becoming a kindergarten teacher is her soul-searching journey to bestow peace and clarity onto her young students and to live up to the calling of her watchful totem deer she encountered many years ago.

The classroom is inspired by Ms. Wapeka's totem deer story, where their mouths burst with excitement to dream and claim their own totem animal.

> "I want a giraffe," a classmate declares.

> "I want a turtle," another classmate declares."

Ms. Wapeka stops the classroom with their continued competitive, ignorant, and naive outburst of totem animals and spirituality.

> "Children," Ms. Wapeka wins the classroom's attention. "Our spirit animals choses us, you do not choose them," she gracefully teaches them.

A docile student raises their hand to question one more concept on Ms. Wapeka's black-colored paper. She calls on them. The student asks about the mesmerizing fiery prism that has been drawn front and center on the black-colored paper. Powerfully illustrated, one's imagination can hear the flames in the void.

> "This is where the magic happens," Ms. Wapeka dazzles. "This is where you happen."

Ms. Wapeka elaborates to finish her concepts and illustrations that the Great Spirit blesses the native people of

Eden with the star's angelic totem animals of wisdom, dreams, and power. Her finger softly taps inside of the fiery prism on the black-colored paper. She concludes that when a native is chosen by their destined totem animal and truly becomes one within it...

> "Not even I can express the pure abounding power of our Great Spirit within this space," Ms. Wapeka veils her illustrating conclusion in heavenly wonderment.

Ms. Wapeka lovingly places her wooden deer totem on her desk.

> "Now it is your turn," Ms. Wapeka calls on a student to share.

> "Dabi." Ms. Wapeka gently calls as she takes a seat on her desk, crossing her legs, and resting her hand on her lap.

Little Dabi Feet answers Ms. Wapeka's call. He leaves his wooden school desk and pitter-patters towards the front of the classroom amongst his peers. Arriving at the front of the chalkboard that has "Who Do You Dream to Be?" written in chalk, Dabi turns around to present his colorful and childish drawing to the classroom. He could not think of a personal totem animal, but he insisted and captured the classroom's attention with a man wearing a cowboy hat of blue, red, and white feathers. The man is covered in a navy-blue poncho with a sheriff-star badge clipped to his heart, brown tactical trousers with a revolver holstered to his right leg, and sturdy wheat-color boots. Dabi proudly points to the man in the drawing.

> "This is my dad," Dabi praises.

> "He looks so cool, Dabi. Tell us what your dad does," Ms. Wapeka rhetorically asks.

Amused, Ms. Wapeka gathers her classroom's childish curiosity, because she already knows what the feathers mean. She is aware the darkness is rising with the sun and is commanding with the moon. It calls for the imminent recruitment of future heroes and the dispatch of blue and red feathers now.

> "My dad is tribal police," Dabi confirms.

Dabi stutters excitably that his father protects the tribes of Tishbe, and Eden, but to the extent Dabi is too immature to know. His father only brought his badge and revolver home, but never the cruel and disturbing reality of Eden. In Dabi's young eyes, that was enough to see his father as a hero and to develop an adolescent heart of honor. Truthfully, it is not Dabi's drawing that paints the picture of his heroic and awesome dad; it is his admiration.

A curious child raises their hand to question the assorted colored feathers on Dabi's father's cowboy hat. The teacher acknowledges the child's curiosity and asks Dabi to explain. One by one, Dabi explains when the blue and red feathers are joined together it means police, and the white feather is "super special." At least, that is how Dabi's father explained it to his little brain. Only Dabi's father bears the white feather in the police.

> "Will your dad give my mom food?" a hungry child ask Dabi.

> "Will your dad help my dad get his job back?" another student ask and interrupts thrillingly.

> "My dad can do anything," Dabi promises.

> "That is inspiring, Dabi. Do you dream to be like your dad?" Ms. Wapeka asks.

Dabi opens his arms as wide as his arms can go to measure how much he dreams of being a protector like his father, but, watching his naïve arms flail with affirmation, an experienced soul knows the torments of Eden and the reality is too physical for silly dreams and passions of a child. Ms. Wapeka, however, believes.

> "Wow, that is really big, Dabi," Ms Wapeka applauds.

> "That is lame," a classmate with an older voice outburst out of turn from the back of the classroom. "You are too weak to ever protect anything," the classmate continues to bully.

Dabi's arms fall by his side, along with his enthusiasm.

> "You are wrong," Dabi rebuts. "I am going to be the greatest protector. Just like my dad," Dabi assures himself.

The bully scoffs. He once upon a time remembers a lit candle during a nightfall dinner. His family, father, and mother were bonding and lavishing him, their only child, Otaktay Inteus. Otaktay's father was celebrated for another flawless and victorious tribal combat. No opponent matched his punching power. He was ruthless and earned a reputation titled "Badger." Otaktay mimicked his father's fighting style by combating an imaginary opponent and spewing punching sounds.

> "That is enough, Otty. Eat your dinner." Otaktay's mother calmly demands.

> "Aww, leave him alone," Otaktay's father defends his son's honor.

Otaktay's father observes all of his son's punching, kicks, grappling, takedowns, headbutts, and then even biting?

> "Whoa, easy there, badger mini-me," Otaktay's father chastises his son to never fight dirty.

> "Yes, you would not want to look silly like your father," Otaktay's mother teases his father's badger combat face paint and funny expressions.

Otaktay's father surrenders to his wife and demands his son stop biting the floor like an animal and eat the candlelight dinner his mother prepared for the family.

> "Besides, if you want to get big and strong like me, you need to eat your food," Otaktay's father encourages. His mother is pleased.

Suddenly, after peaceful moments of candlelight dinner, wolves howl. The pack of wolves howling is intense; it beats the shutters of Otaktay's home. The family is alarmed as Otaktay's father hops from his chair and signals his family to remain quiet as he tries to feel the pack of wolves in an unknown location somewhere outside his home. Otaktay runs into his mother's trembling arms.

> "What are they doing here? They know they are not to cross our borders," Otaktay's mother whispers in fearful frustration.

Otaktay's father panics and throws up his silencing finger to cease his wife's whispering. The wolves will hear. He signals his wife and child to remain in their dining area and away from the windows. They must remain silent as he plans to reach the front door alarm and where his shotgun is mounted. He lightly travels through the hallways and slowly peeks around the corners. Everything appears clear. Only the moonlight cast shadows through the windows as Otaktay's father carefully maneuvers away from them.

Otaktay's father peeks around the last corner of the hallway and observes the front door is still latched. He retrieves his shotgun that is mounted above the door and quickly approaches a drawer containing ammunition and matches. He sets fire to a strand of string by the chimney and watches the sparks slowly burn it. He loads his shotgun, bracing for the door, and opens it cautiously. His shuddering sight forces him to clench his shotgun and the trigger. The moon is full, trespassing and resting on his land. In its brilliant moonlight, it summons three wolves in a formation.

The wolves' eyes are children of the moon, and their bodies resemble the likeness of masculine adult men. A thick mane protects their spiked ears, protruded heads, broad shoulders, forearms, hands, and legs. The smug wolf on the left has its arms crossed, the rabid wolf on the right is drooling, and the alpha wolf in the center leads.

> "Hello," the alpha wolf howls.

The wolves howling besieges anyone who can hear it. A howl that sends a death-cold chill down the spine. Otaktay's father has limited knowledge of the wolves. Most natives do not know much about them. However, he knows they are fast, and strong, and their howls are taunts of aggression.

> "You can not be here, dog," Otaktay's father threatens.

Otaktay's father aims and steadies his shotgun to endanger the wolves to leave. The wolves are not afraid. Instead, the alpha takes a step closer to Otaktay's father. As the alpha hunts Otaktay's father down the center, the other two wolves' formation widens. Otaktay's father is intimidated by their formation and begins to feel powerless as he attempts to retreat inside his home.

Suddenly, a loud whistle launches into the sky from Otaktay's father's chimney. The loud whistle catches the skies and explodes. Bright light briefly flashes the sky above Otaktay's father's home and emits a blue and red exhaust umbrella.

> "They are coming," Otaktay's father relishes.

Otaktay's father's gloating fades as he observes the alpha wolf has stopped and grins.

"But not in time," the alpha wolf taunts.

Otaktay's father frightenedly realizes the wolf formation to the right is gone. However, he is haunted by nerving disguised howls to the right of him, and the smug wolf marches for Otaktay's father.

"Stay back!" Otaktay's father shouts.

Otaktay's father aims his shotgun at the smug marching wolf and fires. Alarmed, Otaktay's father cannot believe the smug wolf did not budge. His powerless shotgun is only a cool breeze for the smug wolf's mane.

"I said stay back!" Otaktay's father shouts desperately.

Otaktay's father fires again, but to no avail. The smug wolf is marching closer. Otaktay's father panics and attempts to reload. He opens his shotgun and tosses away the empty shells. He grabs a couple more shells from his pockets, but unsteadily drops one. He hurries to retrieve the shell from the grass and to finish loading his gun. He is successful. He aims again, and his finger attempts to pull the trigger, but like the sound of a snapping bear trap, the rabid wolf appears in a burst and ravages Otaktay's father's right arm, forcing him to relinquish his shotgun.

Otaktay's father's eyes expand and flicker in terror as he watches his right arm being eaten by the rabid wolf. His last instinct is to punch the rabid wolf with his remaining arm. Desperate to survive, and retreat to his home until the calvary arrives, he attempts a left-handed haymaker. His punching power should give him the time to flee, or at least he thinks. He threw his left-handed haymaker but could not deliver. The smug marching wolf swiftly changes his stance into a four-legged lunge, catching Otaktay's father's left leg. He helplessly screams.

The alpha wolf, with the blink of an eye, faces Otaktay's father and ceases his screams with his claws against his flesh. Otaktay's father's final effort of swinging his left punching fist as hard as he can onto the jaws of the alpha wolf. The alpha wolf laughs, and Otaktay's father shatters his own hand, exposing a bone from his wrist. The alpha wolf snarls with bloodlust and begins to devour Otaktay's father's face. His devouring body falls to the grass. The rapid wolf flings Otaktay's father's right arm and plays with it. The smug wolf stands with Otaktay's left leg in his arms, eating the meat from bones. The alpha wolf devours the remaining corpse of Otaktay's body, and his mangled head rolls down a watery ditch.

Otaktay shoves himself from his mother's trembling arms and to his father's screams.

> "No, Otty. Stop!" Otaktay's mother could not catch her son's irrational escape.

Otaktay sprints through the hallways and observes the wide-open front door. He stops to drag his feet to the entrance. Outside, it is peaceful, and the sound of the wind is soothing. The moonlight is elegant over the grassy terrane. It invites Otaktay to exit his home. He watches his home, but he cannot find his father.

> "Daddy," Otaktay searches.

He searches until his feet make a squish. Otaktay lifts his small shoes to find fresh, clotted blood. He panics and slips facedown into its massacre. Otaktay becomes asthmatic as he continues to panic. Blood covers his eyes. He struggles to find the ditch he knows is always filled with water for the animals. Finding the watery ditch, he splashes his little hands to wash his face. Clean and able to see, Otaktay's heart punches his gut and takes his breath away. Hoping and screaming in circles, Otaktay dances frantically. His chaotic manner attracts his mother and the arriving calvary.

Otaktay lashes out at Dabi that he will be worthless, and be eaten by the wolves, and blames the likes of Dabi's father for failing to protect his father. Otaktay mocks Dabi and his father that they are pigs and causes an "oink" uproar. Otaktay entices the class to laugh with him and at Dabi.

> "That is enough," Ms. Wapeka struggles to gain control of her classroom.

Dabi is embarrassed and feels stranded in the focus of the classroom's mockery. His eyes become softer, and his confidence is like a loyal dog biting its owner.

> "Aww, are you going to cry?" Otaktay instigates.

Ms. Wapeka ejects herself from her desk to confront Otaktay. She arrests his ear and proceeds to yank him out of the classroom.

> "I said that is enough!" Ms. Wapeka dominates.

Unsettling, Otaktay slurs and wrestles with Ms. Wapeka, all while "oinking" at Dabi. Being yanked by the ear, finally on the way out of the classroom, Otaktay kicks the desks and chairs, hurting some of the students, and behaving like a badger.

Little Dabi wipes his tearful memory to become a young man exiting a steamy bathtub. He grabs a towel to cover his waist and another towel to pat his face dry. He approaches the sink but cannot see his reflection in the mirror because of the steam. He clears the steam from the mirror, imprinting a triangular defog, and his golden eyes ponder within the resembling defog prism reflection.

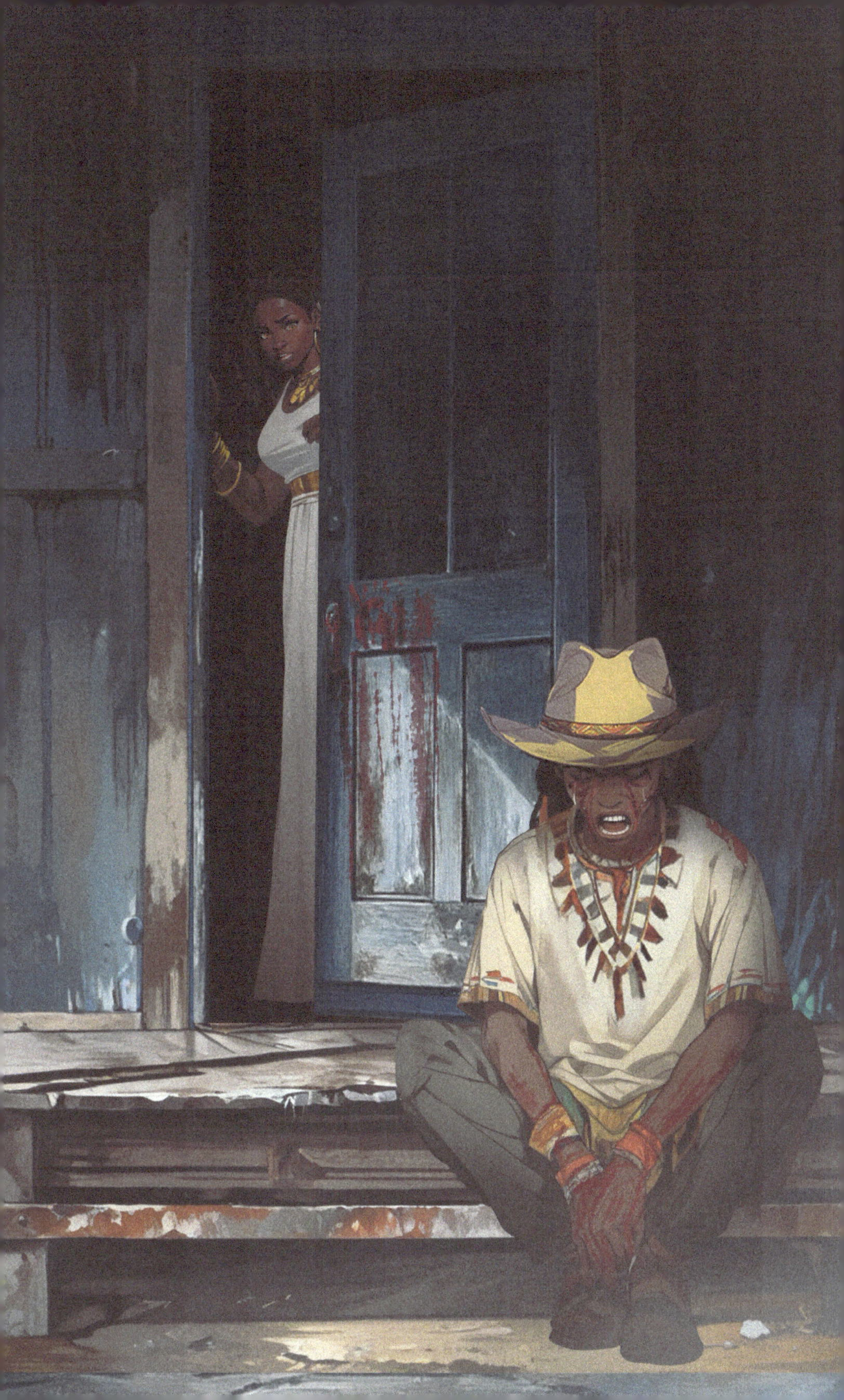

Chapter 2
Wilderness Crimes

Exhausted, bloody fists knock on a door. It smears the door red and awaits to be answered.

> "Mom," a fatigue voice calls.

No one answers. Its shadow sniffles congested blood and coughs it up over the doorway. Too weak to knock again, the shadow leans to the side of the doorway, sits on the ground, and takes a breather against the wooden house. It is Dabi. He contemplates recent events in the rocky wilderness. He does not regret saving the lives of the natives, but heroism continues to conceal itself from him. His punitive emotions mock his self-esteem, like when he once upon a time was bullied as a child. He does not cry, but he wipes crusted blood from the ruptured corner of his eyes and wonders if his actions are all for nothing.

The door opens. While Dabi's vision besets his stupor, his eyes catch a white shape.

> "Oh, Great Spirit! Cub?" a mature woman's voice is shaken.

It is Dabi's mother, Meda Hakan. She is wearing a pure white dress with a golden belt sash around her waist. Her lavishing honey dreadlock hair is charmed in gold jewelry; her arms are strengthened with golden arm cuffing and golden bracelets on her wrists. She hustles to revive her son's condition and puts his exhausted arms around her shoulders. Without the concern of bleeding her pure white dress, she embraces her son to relieve him from the ground.

Meda guides Dabi to a cushioned chair with a broken right arm and broken left leg inside their home.

> "Mom?" Dabi's confusion calls.

Meda arrives back in Dabi after a momentary departure to gather her forest-green medical-grade briefcase. It is engraved with a wheel divided by a four feathered-emblem and embodies four concepts of health and medicine: physical, mental, emotional, and spiritual.

> "I am here, cub," Meda assures.

She grabs a stool to elevate Dabi's feet and nurtures him with water. Holding the cup of water for Dabi to hydrate, Meda carefully tilts the cup of water onto Dabi's lips for him to drink. She sets the cup of water aside to put on gloves and cleanse Dabi's wounds with warm water to reduce his swelling.

> "What happened today, cub?" Meda asks while cleaning the blood from his face.

> "I do not know," Dabi's convictions are misplaced.

Meda finishes cleansing her son's lacerated hands.

> "This may be uncomfortable, Cub," Meda comforting warns.

She sterilizes the area with iodine derived from fish around the wounds on Dabi's hands to protect him from infection and retrieves a sterile needle and thread from her medical briefcase. Minutes pass, and Meda finishes suturing Dabi's wounds. She places an ice pack on Dabi's head to cool him, and he now regains some strength to hydrate himself.

> "Your color is coming back," Meda proudly admits as she caresses his face.

Dabi continues to hydrate himself now that his strength is better. However, he coddles both of his hands. His palms are sore, and trying to hold anything is agonizing. Meda observes Dabi's discomfort while she tidies the medical mess.

> "When you get some rest, you are going to tell me what happened today," Meda asserts.

In the meantime, Meda instructs her son to rest. She helps Dabi to finally stand up from the cushioned and broken chair and holds him to be sure he is stable enough to walk. She guides Dabi to his bedroom and lays him on his bed, pulling the covers over him. His mother's comfort is a remedy.

> "I am going to start dinner," Meda shares.

Dabi insists he helps his mother with the cooking. To include himself with the delicious aroma of their home and the satisfaction of his family's appetite. He sits up with desperate enthusiasm to recover his will from rock bottom disappointment. Searching for identity and purpose, he clings on to the hope of his mother's permission to feel a snippet of self-confidence.

> "You cannot even hold a spoon to stir the sauce, cub" Meda refuses with a quip, but it strikes Dabi subtly.

Meda is confident in her cooking, but a bit overprotective of the kitchen. Her hands were not born for just medical care, but for culinary as well.

> "After all, that is why your father married me, "Meda winks with her humor.

> "Where is father?" Dabi asks.

Dabi's disappointment continues to search from his dead-end heartbreak. Meda stands to exit Dabi's room. She stops at the doorway of his bedroom and explains he was called in for an unexpected incident.

"What incident?" Dabi is hesitant to ask.

Meda does not know the details of her husband's job situation, but all she knows is that it is a crime scene of some kind, and every available officer has been called to investigate.

"Where?" Dabi asks with a nauseous stomach.

Meda confirms the crime scene is somewhere on the outskirts of Tishbe.

"The rocky wilderness I believe," Meda remembers. "Get some rest," She leaves with a smile, but Dabi is restless.

Sturdy wheat-color boots smash the ground in the rocky wilderness and kick up dirt while demounting from its golden stallion. Its navy-blue poncho, hanging from the waist, enters an active crime scene of forensic teams, officers of Tishbe tribes, and coroners. The windy environment blows blue, red, and white feathers from its cowboy hat to float beside its holstered revolver and brown tactical trousers. Finally, its sheriff-star badge clipped to its heart is respectfully greeted as Abraham Hakan.

> "This place looks like a warzone," sheriff Hakan observes to himself.

A young man, a little older than Dabi, approaches and greets Abraham at the active crime scene. He is mature for his youth, and advanced. He wears a band of feathers, red and blue, around his head. His sleeveless vest of blue and white patterns represents his tribe, and his right shoulder is imprinted with talons. His gloves reveal he is a master archer, and of course, his quiver, arrows, and bow.

> "Nice to meet you, sheriff. My name is Elsu Hania," he greets.

Abraham and Elsu join hands. Abraham remembers Elsu Hania's name. He was to train him within the following week. Elsu informs Abraham that because of sudden unforeseen circumstances, his orientation was expedited. Abraham compliments Elsu that he was impressed with his resume and his expertise is unique for officers of Tishbe. However, one detail confuses him. Another name was listed on Elsu's Hania's resume that he cannot remember.

> "So, what have you learned here?" sheriff Hakan investigates.

Elsu updates several craters and destruction in the rocky wilderness. The plants and trees have been crushed. Leaves, twigs, sticks, and branches are scattered. Mountains have been destroyed, and pillars drill the land. So far, the only signs of life are the birds and critters in their interrupted habitat.

> "That is quite the eye you have there," sheriff Hakan is impressed."

Elsu admires the generous compliment from Abraham, but he cannot take all the credit for the geographical information. Elsu whistles, and from the skies, with a gust of wind, a vulture yaps and descends on Elsu's right shoulder. The blonde shaggy feathers resemble a mane for the vulture. Its yellow-gold wings could blow a boar's eyes closed, and its beak could scuff concrete.

> "Sheriff, meet Lion," officer Hania proudly introduces.

Abraham is surprised by the Lion's size and impressed Elsu tamed it. He now remembers the one forgotten detail of Elsu's resume. It was not a typo from a typewriter or a human error. Elsu accurately tamed a beast that has expertise in stealth, exploration, and tracking. Their companionship is dated for years and a brief history of Elsu's totem testimony and background. Abraham again welcomes Elsu to the team and proceeds with their active crime investigation.

> "Any evidence of landmines in the area?" sheriff Hakan investigates.

> "Hang on to your hat," officer Hania cautions the sheriff.

Elsu releases Lion to sweep the crime scene for further information. It gusts from Elsu's shoulder, and Abraham protects his hat from the blast of wind. Elsu's feedback is that there is no evidence of shrapnel. Abraham watches several investigative teams carelessly investigate the terrain.

> "You are right, someone would have detonated one by now," sheriff Hakan agrees.

Abraham investigates the forensics team, while Elsu investigates the coroner team. The forensics team presents newly discovered data to Abraham. Footprints in their area determined there were eleven suspects, and evaluating the boot sizes of the footprints, there were eight men and three women.

> "I am assuming they were all natives?" Sheriff Hakan deduces.

The forensics team cannot conclude, however, based on their historical facts, that dogs of Eden are forbidden to cross their borders. Therefore, in theory, the only suspects who could be responsible for the destruction of their land are the outlaws.

> "Sheriff, over here!" Officer Hania flags.

Elsu flags for Abraham's leadership. His call is urgent as he shouts and waves from the coroner's team and where Lion yaps. Abraham responds to Elsu's urgent call along with other officers of Tishbe and the forensic team. They gather for Elsu and the coroner team to investigate Lion's new evidence. The lion's wings flap over the evidence of blood.

Abraham, Elsu, officers of Tishbe, the coroner team, and the forensics team are paralyzed.

> "Is that blood?" a traumatized voice breaks through their huddle.

A native in a suit, tie, and cufflinks breaks through Abraham, Elsu, officers of Tishbe, the coroner team, and the forensic team. His presence is superior, and his involvement is feared. He demands confirming evidence of whose blood it is and right now. Elsu recognizes the native as a civilian, so he attempts to confront him. Abraham deters Elsu's lawful code of conduct with a headshake of discretion. He whispers that he is Pilan Tate.

> "Now tell me. Whose blood is that?" Pilan Tate demands.

The coroners evaluate the state of the blood to conclude that whichever blood it is, it is dead, but cannot factually confirm if it is native or something else. Abraham observes subtle holes in the dirt and instructs the forensic team to carefully dust excess dirt from the holes without compromising the potential evidence. One of the members of the forensics team questions Abraham's reasoning, because, due to the rocky wilderness' condition, holes are common.

> "You challenge the order of a sheriff?" Pilan Tate is offended. "You are done," he releases the combative member of the forensics team.

Tension inflicts Elsu, the forensic team, the coroner team, and the officers of Tishbe as they helplessly watch the defeated member's rejection of the forensics team. Abraham resents Pilan's decision to casually destroy someone's livelihood. He has witnessed too many natives' livelihoods trouble to ruin, and with the foresight, it will hurt Eden in the end.

> "What are you staring for? Get me my evidence," Pilan Tate threatens.

The forensic team proceeds to follow Abraham's instructions, and in a matter of minutes, more small holes in a five-count pattern unveil themselves, and a larger hole in the center of the smaller ones. The more the forensics team unveils the evidence, they discover profound evidence. Abraham, Elsu Pilan, officers of Tishbe, the forensic team, and the coroner team analyze the holes that have sharp edges. They are paw prints.

> "No," sheriff Hakan succumbs to denial.

> "This is outrageous," Pilan Tate is violated.

> "Those do not belong to bears," officer Hania acknowledges sarcastically.

Abraham comes to terms with the prints belonging to the dogs of Eden. A debate arises in their huddle. Elsu asserts that the dogs of Eden have not been seen across their borders in twenty years and denies their treason now makes sense. Pilan retorts to Elsu with the perspective that the dogs of Eden could be roaring for a rebellion. Eden's history documents it happened one hundred years ago. Eden must brace for the possibility of an uprising.

A member of the coroner team optimistically suggests that the evidence of the blood could mean a dog of Eden is dead. An officer of Tishbe agrees with the member of the coroner team and theorizes that the evidence of eleven native footprints ambushed a dog of Eden for trespassing.

"You mean this could be blood by a dog of Eden?" sheriff Hakan seeks understanding.

Abraham is a little skeptical, but he agrees it does appear the way they see it for now.

"We should be celebrating, then," Pilan Tate cheers.

"Wait! Look. There is more," officer Hania directs everyone's attention to more tracks leading towards the mountain.

Abraham leads Elsu, officers of Tishbe, Pilan, the forensic team, and the coroner team to the mountain.

"Look. Another footprint," officer Hania reveals.

The forensics team studies the new evidence of another footprint pattern. They conclude that the boot size belongs to another man.

"And there's more blood," officer Hania examines and is disgruntled

Abraham separates himself from Elsu and the teams towards the edge of the mountain. He takes a deep breath to relieve himself of the environment's taunting tension and confusion to rationalize the best approach for understanding the unknown outcome of their evidence. Abraham constructs the acquired evidence of the boot prints, the animal prints, and the blood. He spins around to face Elsu and the teams with determination.

> "Officer Hania," sheriff Hakan leads. "Get Lion to scent every trace of blood here in this wilderness. If whoever or whatever has been involved here, we will track the scent back to town."

> "Yes, sir." officer Hania's attitude echos sheriff Hakan's determination and leads with Lion down the mountain.

Abraham instructs the forensics team to gather blood samples for testing and to duplicate them at their lab.

> "I want to know if it's human blood or something else," sheriff Hakan instructs.

Abraham points to a native photographer who is involved with the forensics team to take pictures of the animal footprints. He requests personal copies of the photos for further investigation, and finally instructs the rest of the forensics team to investigate the excavation equipment for prints, hair, and other possible evidence to help their investigation.

Abraham dismisses the team while Pilan approaches him.

> "Be sure to keep me informed of any and every new evidence you will discover, Sheriff. I will make sure our white feathers are ready " Pilan Tate bear arms.

Pilan departs and leaves Abraham with intimidation of Eden's future.

Abraham and his stallion gallop home to rest his feathers. He opens the door where he is greeted with the aroma of supper and soon a kiss from his wife, Meda.

> "Something smells amazing," Abraham excitably compliments after a stressful day.

"How was the wilderness?" Meda asks Abraham as she caresses his hands and wrists on the kitchen table. He follows his wife to the kitchen and briefly explains the limited information he has learned in the wilderness. Baffled, he messages his forehead to contemplate the possibility of wilderness crimes aloud with his wife and invites her help for the unknown identification of new animalistic prints as he waits for the forensic team's photo evidence.

> "Do you think it's prints from the dogs of Eden?" Meda asks with concernment.

Abraham's experience denies, or at least is skeptical, that the prints belong to the dogs of Eden. Their prints are large and heavy.

> "These new footprints are bigger," Abraham explains, but also malnourished.

Abraham cheers up to introduce his new trainee, Elsu Hania, and his companion, Lion.

He describes the Lion's powerful wingspan and titan intimidation. Pleased the police have recruited such a talented young man, Abraham shares some details of Elsu's first mission to investigate.

> "Speaking of 'talent,' where are my sons?" Abraham seeks.

Meda confirms their oldest son, David, is out in town rehearsing a new song with Kenya while Dabi is in bed asleep. Confused, Abraham watches the clock to realize it is too early for bed.

> "No, it's too early to be in bed," Abraham says with dissatisfaction.

Abraham gets up from the chair at the kitchen table to wake up Dabi, but Meda ends his approach.

> "Wait! Let him rest," Meda pleads to her husband.

Frustrated, Abraham recognizes Meda's sincere deter and informs her he will have a discussion of Dabi's future. Abraham grieves for Dabi's current path in life and is concerned about his actions. Desperate to spare Dabi from futility, Abraham will guard Dabi's future from the life of vagabond savages.

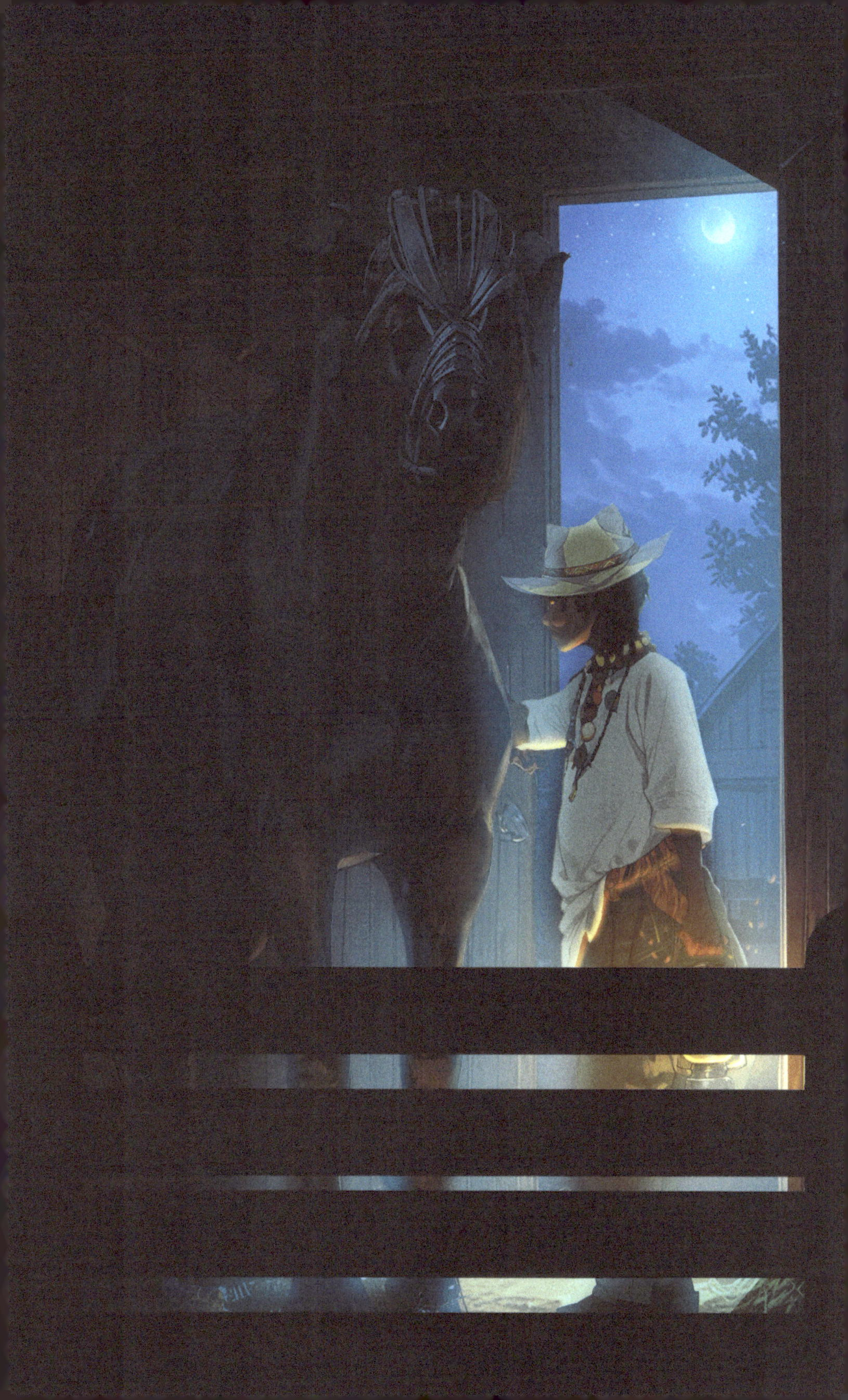

Chapter 3
Ride Of Resistance

Dabi jolts himself awake due to the throbbing pain in his hands. He holds up his stitched hands and is reminded of the failure in the wilderness. Frustrated, he feels he is back to square one. Eventually, relaxing his arms, Dabi sighs with the burden he can still accomplish a sacrificial offering to pardon Eden's and his people's suffering.

> "But the stone is destroyed," Dabi contemplates.

Dabi considers going back to the wilderness, because maybe there are fragments of the stone, but he can still hope to sacrifice to appease the gods. He improvises to ensure his personal task is succeeded and concludes he will ride out during nightfall to elude unwanted attention that could get him arrested. Raising up both his stitched hands again, he briefly glances at them and clenches with morale and diligence.

> "Alright, no more whining," Dabi restores.

Dabi removes himself from his sheets and leaves his bed to exit his room, where the hallway greets him with the aroma of a finished dinner prepared by his mother. He follows the scent to the kitchen, where his father, mother, and brother are sitting at the table.

> "Right on time, boy," Abraham's tone suggesting consequences for unpunctuality.

> "I'm sorry," Dabi apologizes while hiding his hands from his father.

> "I'm glad you're up, cub," Meda reassures.

Dabi takes his seat at the table where his meal is already prepared. He favors his hands in a way to conceal his injuries, hoping the rest of his family does not take notice and to avoid questions.

> "How are you doing, bro?" David embraces Dabi, his little brother with enthusiasm. Almost singing as he does it.

> "You know, just living the dream," Dabi evades with sarcasm.

Dabi eats with his head, staring down at his plate and fiddles with his food, loathing the idea of being useless. His lack of fulfillment besets inferiority, especially when he compares himself to his brother's talents, David, and yearns for his father's respect.

> "Speaking of dreams, how'd the rehearsal go?" Meda discusses.

Joyful to elaborate, David expresses his girlfriend, Kenya, and himself have been practicing their rehearsals at random villages of native homes to uplift their spirits with hope and peace. Some of their rehearsals were sponsored by generous food vendors. Many natives, a few families, and some villages have been inspired, and fed with bread, meat, and dairy.

> "That's amazing, son," Abraham is proud.

Abraham is proud his eldest son, David, is becoming prevalent with his music and generosity in Eden, and to emulate his father's role of compassion, duty, sacrifice, and respect. His hope is to see his children follow the ideals of servitude and offerings of courage and integrity amid Eden's wolves with eyes of the moon, betrayal from the native people, and the path of resistance.

David's demeanor, however, suddenly becomes haunted when he shares some homes in a village called Baraga, Kenya, and he appears ritualistic. When they knocked, no one answered, but there were horses in the stable. Kenya encouraged David to knock again, because they had bread, meat, and dairy to donate. David attempted to knock again, but before he could, the door squeaked and opened slightly. Inside were lit candles with shadows, symbols on the walls, and a larger symbol on the floor where an altar had been assembled.

> "Rituals are common in Eden, son," Abraham is undisturbed.

> "That's right. I'm sure those tribes are just worshipping," Meda confirms.

David respectfully rebuts. He continues the story of his encounter with Kenya, where once the door opened slightly, a blind eye and a rotting face greeted them. Moments of disturbing silence, the blind eye did not blink, and its face did not speak. David and Kenya were too timid to move, like the feeling a rapid dog will chase after you if you make a sudden move or flee. Kenya cautiously protected herself over David's shoulder while he cautiously placed the bread, meat, and dairy by the doorway. David and Kenya retreated to their horses while the blind eye continued to haunt them as they departed.

Abraham is aware of Eden's grieving stomach, sparse remedies, poverty, and unjustified gun smoke increasing in many areas of Eden. Families, villages, and tribes are suffering, and too many are taking matters into their own hands – some for grace, but most for corruption. Their ritualistic practices are their virtue to appease the gods. The performances of dancing and chanting are usually uplifting and elegant. Abraham accesses David's testimony that maybe that poor native needs a doctor or at least a wellness check.

"I will have my new rookie take a look," Abraham accepts David's unsettling concerns.

"How awesome is that? Is he cool?" David asks his father about his new trainee.

Abraham is proud to admit his new trainee is a talented young man with much potential, and boasting with admiration of his beast companion's wings, beak, talons, power, and tracking skills. He acknowledges that Elsu is just the kind of young man in law enforcement Tishbe, Eden needs, and is confident of Elsu's youth, unique abilities, new pair of eyes for crime, devotion, strength, and stamina.

"I can't wait to find out what this kid is truly made of," Abraham anticipates.

Abraham's discontent pivots and engages Dabi's preoccupied slouch. Observing his son fiddling with his food and not participating with the family compels him to challenge Dabi's unpredictable path because, as a sheriff veteran, Abraham is aware of the epidemic of outlaws and vagabonds. However, as a father, Abraham is restless for the possibility Dabi would be persuaded to their ideals and their bandanna likeness.

Dabi is annoyed by another intervention from his father. He knows life has not honored him with purpose, esteem, or talent, and to be perpetually lectured that he still needs to find it or at least work on it. Dab justifies that he is indeed trying to find his purpose and become skillful, but Abraham sharply disapproves. In his eyes, Abraham is offended and does not trust his son is doing anything towards a promising future.

Dabi is angered that he is being chastised by his father and to be secluded in mediocrity. He feels it is almost pointless to argue with his father and his fervent attempt to gain favor from him, especially since he never wins any decency. Abraham compels Dabi to find work in Eden that could guide him to the discovery of duty and skill, because maybe the final resort is a life lesson that will shepherd Dabi to a rite of passage. Abraham's tone, unfortunately, almost implies that Dabi is a disappointment, a failure, and a shame to the Hakan family.

Meda reaches for Abraham's shoulder to relieve him of his relentless charge against Dabi. David stops eating because of the uproar and tension. He feels sympathy for his little brother and wishes life was better for him. Dabi stands up from his chair fiercely, restraining himself from offending his family any further, and storms out of their ranch with his cowboy hat in his hand. David is saddened, Meda is heart-stricken, and Abraham is feeling guilty.

Dabi pushes open the sliding doors of the barn and enters his family's stable, where he approaches his black and brown horse, Rottweiler. It neighs and snorts with excitement as Dabi gathers Rottweiler's saddle and bridle to unleash him.

> "Whoa, settle down, buddy," Dabi controls Rottweiler as he unleashes him from the stable.

Dabi pulls his cowboy hat over his head and mounts Rottweiler. He takes a deep breath and a moment's glance at his home before he departs, because uncertainty begins to challenge his judgement that he is making the right decision even though he is being hasty. He turns away from his home to notice his hands are trembling while grasping onto Rottweiler's reins. Rottweiler feels his owner's hesitation, and so, he neighs. He shakes Dabi out of his hesitation and doubting daydreaming. Now, he focuses and decides on his path with a genuine decision.

> "Did you have to be that hard on him?" Meda asks while wiping a tear from her eye.

Abraham, remorsefully, explains he does not want his son to become another statistical victim of an outlaw or vagabond by means of tough love, but Meda disproves this.

> "Where's the love?" Meda tearfully challenges.

Meda agrees with her husband that tough love is necessary, but for Dabi, it is not love; it appears to be contempt. She sends David outside to find Dabi. He leaves in a hurry to find his little brother and is worried. After moments of Meda expressing her heartache and disapproval of her husband's remorseful reasoning and parenting skills, David returns with an alarm.

> "He's gone," David exclaims.

Abraham rises from his chair to approach the front door where his cowboy hat of blue, red, and white feathers is hanging.

> "Where are you going?" Meda asks and de-escalates.

Abraham continues to dress, lacing up his sturdy wheat-color boots, throwing on his navy-blue poncho, and clipping his sheriff-star badge onto his chest. Finally, he pulls his cowboy hat of blue, red, and white feathers over his head.

> "To find my son," Abraham affirms.

Dabi and Rottweiler ride miles away from villages, taverns, and towns to the outskirts of the rocky wilderness. He is determined for life to bestow favor and purpose for him. His soul-searching endeavor for prevalence and Eden's prosperity. However, he halts Rottweiler's gallop due to commotions. Dabi demounts from Rottweiler's saddle and hides him in the shadows to investigate the commotions off into the distance.

Traveling from every hiding spot he can find as he becomes closer to the commotion; Dabi's eyes finally peek over a stonewall to witness native police gathering evidence. He observes the native police retrieving a corpse from the crater and rubble right where he needs to find the stone's fragments. Dabi fully conceals himself with his back against the stonewall in frustration because it seems his motivations are always rebuked.

> "Dammit!" Dabi exclaims.

Suddenly, like a knee-jerking reaction, Dabi swings his arm and slams his fist against the stonewall, provoking the native police's alertness. Dabi is in shock and disbelief at what he has done. He cautiously peeks over the stonewall again to know if he has ruined his discretion, but this time to catch an officer approaching his location with a trained revolver in one hand and a torch in the other hand.

Dabi panics and predicts two possibilities if he runs, because if he does, he knows he will be arrested, or worse, shot on site. The officer's torch becomes closer, and it is time for Dabi to act now. He shuts his eyes and grabs his head to think and act quickly. He knows if the officer arrests him, he will certainly bring shame to not only his father, but his Hakan name. Dabi opens his eyes to scan his small area without being seen to discover one thing, a rock from the rubble.

> "Over here! I think I found something," an officer alerts a small team of officers to Dabi's compromised position.

The officer takes a brief cover to spin around the stonewall with his torch and trained revolver, but Dabi is not there to be seen. The officer, confused, signals the small team of officers that the situation is a false alarm, and holsters his weapon, until he spots Dabi.

> "Intruder!" the officer shouts.

The officer, alarmed, attempts to draw his revolver to shoot Dabi, but the officer is knocked bloody unconscious. Dabi hurls the rock at the officer's head he gained from the rubble in the area and desperately escapes with crying, fear, and panic. Every officer in the wilderness chases after Dabi, but he has the advantage of a head start. However, Dabi's head start advantage does not stop the rest of the officers from shooting at him. A lead bullet finds Dabi's thigh, forcing him to stumble and hop while applying pressure to his wound to control the bleeding with his hand.

Dabi manages to mount Rottweiler for an escape. Unfortunately, Rottweiler neighs in pain after being caught in a crossfire. Overwhelmed by events, Dabi and Rottweiler escape without any more gunfire injuries. Dabi and Rottweiler gallop urgently as they are being chased for miles by the native police. Their strategized formation, training, and relentless gunfire overcome Dabi's and Rottweiler's path. The trained officers' gunfire barricades Dabi and Rottweiler from fleeing back to Tishbe; instead, rapid-fire forces them to detour to environmental resistances and enemy borders.

Dabi and Rottweiler are struck again with lead bullets. Dabi is hit in the shoulder, and Rottweiler is hit in the hip. The relentless pursuit of the native police's rapid gunfire and devastating injuries blasts Dabi and Rottweiler to stumble over ditches, rocks, uneven terrain, and abandoned carriages. Quickly losing control against every resistance, swerving left and swerving right, Dabi and Rottweiler slip and tumble down a steep cliff and into a murky valley. The native police halt their relentless pursuit above ground as they observe Dabi and Rottweiler disappear.

Some time passes as Dabi wakes up, and his vision lags to return. He struggles to sit up from the cold ground while pampering his wounded shoulder and leg. Looking around, he cannot locate Rottweiler. The valley is too dark. Not even daylight could save his sight. Anxious to find Rottweiler, Dabi refuses to wait for his eyes to adjust to the murky valley. He whistles for Rottweiler's wellbeing, and nearby, Rottweiler whines. Like sonar, Dabi continues to whistle, leading him to Rottweiler's neighing distress.

Dabi blindly touches and glides his hands in the dark valley until he touches and finds Rottweiler. He hears Rottweiler panting and caresses his muzzle. Eventually,

Dabi feels something wet and sticky on Rottweiler's neck. He brings his hand close to his face to notice the wet, sticky substance, which is blood. Frightened, Dabi glides his hand to find the source of the blood until he touches Rottweiler's belly to discover a bleeding gunshot wound.

> "No, why is this happening to me?" Dabi weeps.

Dabi desperately applies pressure on Rottweiler's belly to control the bleeding. However, Rottweiler's breathing becomes shallow.

> "Please stay with me, buddy," Dabi pleads.

Dabi cannot control Rottweiler's bleeding gunshot wound. Terror overcomes him as his eyes fill with tears and frustration. Suddenly, Dabi's vision becomes blurry again, and his strength to apply pressure on Rottweiler's gunshot wound weakens. He evaluates his bleeding shoulder from the gunshot and realizes his wound has worsened. Death and sorrow arrest his mentality. He bawls to the heavens and faints.

More time passes, and Dabi awakens with a headache on a padded cot inside a deserted cabin. He realizes his shoulder and leg have been sutured and his gunshot wounds repaired. His adjusting eyes scan the deserted cabin to catch the moon looking at him from the shadows.

"Wakey-wakey, golden eye," a stranger howl and greets Dabi.

Dabi flings himself against a corner in fear of the stranger. He acknowledges the stranger's brown fur, leather jacket, his eyes resembling the moon, his sharp nails, and pointy teeth.

"You're a..." Dabi stutters.

The stranger, sitting on a crate, picks at his pointy canines with his sharp thumb and removes a piece of meat from his teeth.

"Hi, I'm Beko," he introduces himself with smirky confidence.

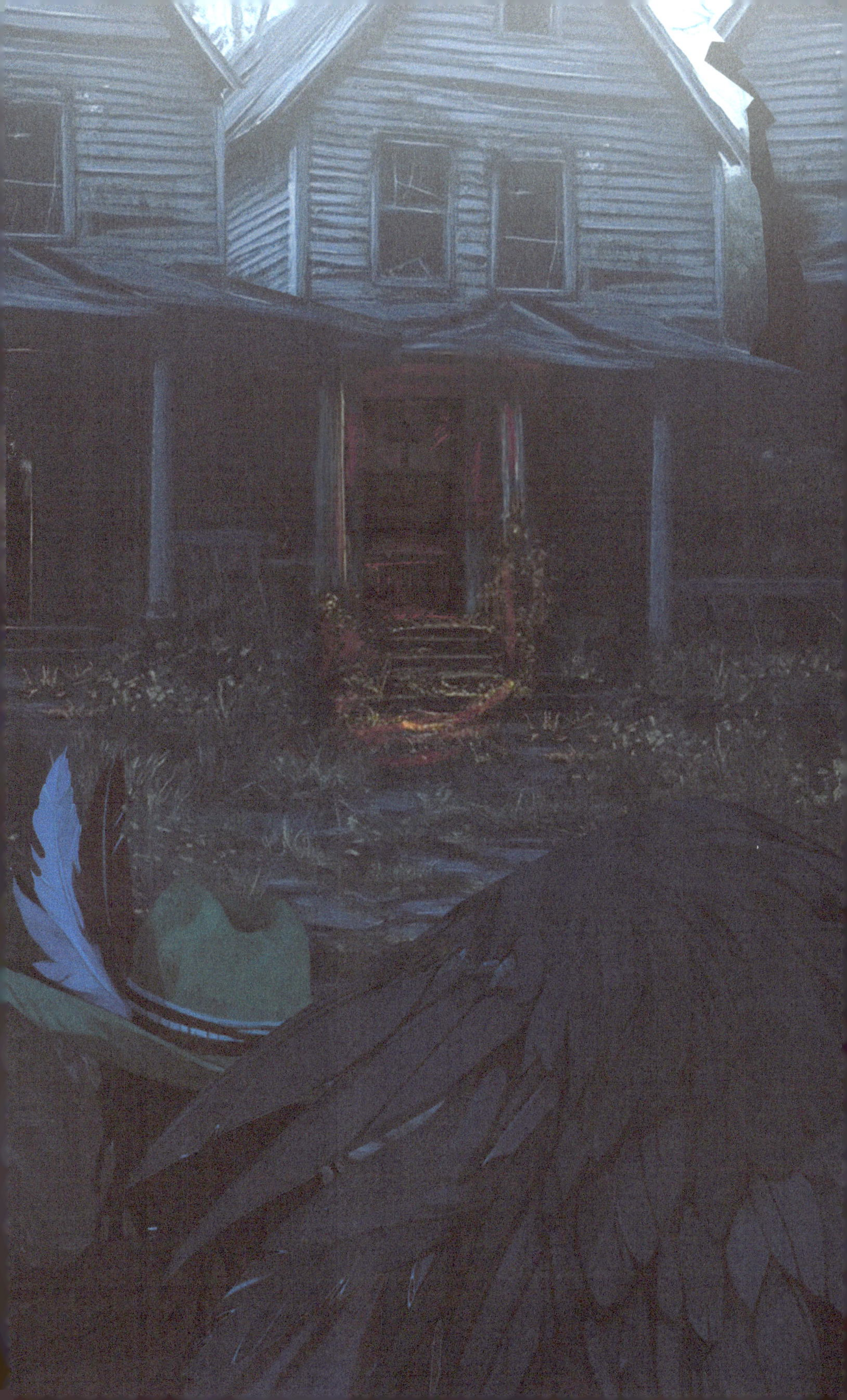

Short Story
Elsu Hania

Blue skies at sunrise and an early morning breeze glide the Lion through an open window from the ceiling. It dives and lands on the headboard of Elsu's bed, hovering over him. Lion flaps its wings, spawning a gust, and yaps Elsu awake.

"Five more minutes," Elsu argues.

Elsu catches his coverings from blowing away by Lion's wings. He pulls his coverings over his head, but Lion pecks it away from his grasp.

"Ouch," Elsu flinches to Lion's pecking. "Okay, I'm up," Elsu concedes.

Elsu, not an early bird, struggles to get out of bed. He eventually sits up, legs hanging over the edge of the bed, and rewards Lion with a treat.

"Let's get us some breakfast," Elsu leads Lion.

Elsu stands as Lion nests onto his shoulder. He approaches the living room, where he is greeted by his twin brother, Etu, listening to the news on the antenna radio. Elsu's genuine curiosity questions why his brother is still at home.

> "Aren't you going to be late for work?" Elsu asks.

Etu being an early riser for delivering common goods to merchants in Eden, Elsu guesses if his brother has been fired from the company. Etu denies this but confides in Elsu his routine delivery route has increased in gang activity that is calling themselves "Badgers." Worrisome, Etu considers quitting the company for the sake of his life. However, Elsu rejects his brother's concerns and encourages him to continue his route.

> "We must be courageous," Elsu encourages. "For their memory"

Etu doubts. He shares with his brother he is not heroic like him and is not convinced what he does is worth his sacrifice. Elsu approaches his brother and gives him a brotherly jab on the chest.

> "You'll find your way," Elsu promises.

And if Etu does not, Elsu says he will shoot him with an arrow. Etu surrenders and agrees to go back to work for the sake of his parents' memory and not to be shot by his brother's arrow.

> "Aren't you going to work too?" Etu asks.

Elsu answers that he is needed in Baraga. Elaborating, the sheriff has recently given him a new assignment for a wellness checkup about a man who may be sick, but his tone speaks with apathy. Anxious to resume the wilderness crimes investigation, or as he calls it, "the big leagues," Elsu feels his new assignment is a lame, glorified house call.

Etu humbles Elsu that everyone must start somewhere, but Elsu shares that he always dreamed of being involved with horse chases, gunfire, bow hunting, and true action combat like the western stories from theatric stage plays their father and mother used to take Etu and himself when they were children. Whimsically, Etu hopes his brother lives up to his dreams and is caught in a crosshair. Etu mimics a shooting gun expression at his brother with his hand as he leaves for work, and Elsu returns their brotherly gesture.

"Ready to go, Lion?" Elsu prepares for his officer duties.

Officer Hania demounts from his horse in Baraga. He looks around cautiously and observes the village, which appears abandoned, while tumbleweeds are blown past him.

"Scout," Officer Hania commands.

Lion yaps and takes off to the skies from Officer Hania's shoulder. Officer Hania pulls out a pad with an address. As he searches for the correct residence, he notices a resident suspiciously closing their door. On guard, Officer Hania eventually locates the residence. He approaches the door and repeatedly announces himself. There is no answer, but the door is not locked. He opens the door and announces himself one more time before entering, but again, no response.

However, he quickly draws his bow and arrow for the discovery of blood. Before he proceeds through the house any further, he verbally commands any suspects to show themselves. Moments pass, but just an eerie silence appears. As Officer Hania continues his search, he observes a wooden altar, bones in jars, and a bowl of blood. Eventually, during more moments of investigating, Officer Hania discovers a bloody footprint. He pulls out a sketch of the wilderness drawn by a forensics team member and compares it to the unknown monstrous footprint.

Officer Hania is troubled. The bloody footprint matches the bloody footprint in the sketch. He fears the dogs of Eden have committed treason because what other kind of animal match the mysterious bloody footprint? Hesitant, Officer Hania knows his newfound evidence could be the beginning of an all-out war.

Milton Keynes UK
Ingram Content Group UK Ltd.
UKHW051841151124
451187UK00007B/86